Ravenshire

R.L. Caudill

Ravenshire Copyright © 2013 R.L. Caudill

Published by Full Moon Publishing, LLC

Glade Spring, VA

Webiste http://www.fullmoonpublishingllc.com/

ISBN: 0615795161
ISBN-13: 978-0615795164

Edited by Jamie White and CP Bialois
Beta reader MD Martin

Cover photo purchased from Shutterstock

DEDICATION

To my wonderful family whose love and support inspire me
to write. I love you Ricky, Brittany, Nikita and Travis.

CONTENTS

The Town

Ravenshire was a tiny hamlet pressed against the rim of the ocean. The town was quaint in its small-minded ways with back fence gossips and rumor mills that quickly turned even the most minute detail into a whopper of a story.

Ravenshire being pressed against the ocean rim on one side and being nestled amongst plush, emerald mountains and cool, rushing streams on the other three was black with ravens. As the ravens graced the treetops and looked down over the town in dismay they bore witness to the goings-on in the community. They made continuous circles in the sky, lounged on the rooftops, and pranced around on the velvet grass. They were everywhere the eye could see, and even places that weren't visible to the human eye. It was as if they were keeping watch over something in the tiny, eccentric town.

The ravens had been there as long as anyone could remember; in fact, the ravens settled Ravenshire before people did and no one knew why the ravens were there except for the Frye family.

Up on a small embankment in this whimsical town sat a small, white wood-frame church. The church had three stained glass windows, each depicting a biblical scene. A small steeple sat atop the building right in the middle of the roof. A tiny porch was attached to the front with a modest-sized brass bell hanging just to the left. The church was built over a swiftly flowing creek that made everyone quite drowsy during Sunday morning service. Inside sat thirty wooden pews—fifteen on each side. Brass gas lamps lined the side walls, casting eerie shadows that danced and swayed on the walls. A pulpit presided at the end of the aisle in full view of the only entrance to the building. The door was at the back of the church behind the pews.

Even though it was never admitted by Preacher Norris, everyone in Ravenshire knew the reason there was only one door. It was so no one in the good congregation could sneak out in the middle of a sermon. Preacher Norris wanted to make sure that everyone in the congregation benefited from the full extent of his lengthy sermons.

Ravenshire was a simple town and was not very wealthy. Most of the good people of the town gave as many tithes as they could, and Preacher Norris' attention to detail in the church never went unnoticed. Long, luxurious, red, plush carpeting ran the length of the aisle.

No one dared to question the good pastor about the exorbitant costs of the stained glass windows or the rich carpeting, as they all dreaded his lecture that God was worth every penny spent on *his* house. Instead, the good people kept their thoughts a secret and continued to dip into their threadbare pockets to give to the church promising them ever-lasting life.

McMurray's Mercantile stood in the center of the town, a fact that was frowned upon by Preacher Norris. In his opinion, the church should have been in the center but, alas, it had been built long before he became pastor in Ravenshire. As it was, the McMurrays had two very spoiled children—one girl, Emilia, and one boy, Rosten.

Emilia had long, stringy, blonde hair and sly green eyes that were similar to the eyes of the local stray cat. She was tall and lanky and had big feet. She was two years older than her brother, Rosten, and loved to lord it over him. She was mean to him, which is probably why Rosten was in turn mean to others. Everyone in town said he was so mischievous because of his red hair and freckles.

Once, Emilia caught him in the outhouse and propped a shovel under the door handle. Rosten was locked in with the stench and the flies for three hours before anyone realized he was missing. It had been an extremely hot day and by the time they found him, Rosten didn't smell well at all. His mother gave him a huge bar of lye soap and sent him to the creek. She sternly suggested he not return until he and his clothing were thoroughly free from the wretched odor that clung to him like the flies on the waste in that outhouse.

Rosten was a petit boy with fiery red hair and big, round, green eyes. He didn't just have a few freckles, he had freckles all over his body. He was always pulling some type of prank on his sister. As a matter of fact, he didn't discriminate as he pulled pranks on everyone. They weren't your everyday funny practical jokes; these were vicious, mean escapades.

Once, he spent a half a day looking for the perfect frog. When he found it, he stealthily snuck it into the church before service one Sunday morning while everyone was congregating out in the yard saying their *"hellos"* and *"how are yous?"*

He took the frog in and climbed up onto the rafter directly above the pulpit, right where Preacher Norris would stand to give his Sunday morning damnation-if-you-don't-do-better services. While everyone was either deep in concentration on the preacher's words, in a deep sleep because of the sermon, or dozing due to the lulling stream under the church—just before the damnation-if-you-don't-do-better bit—the dirty, gnarled frog took one gigantic leap. It landed on top of the preacher's head with a hind leg in one of Preacher Norris' ears and a front leg in his mouth.

After service, Rosten got his own lengthy damnation-if-you-don't-do-better preaching from good old

Preacher Norris. When he got home, his father gave him a good old-fashioned thrashing. Then his mother did the preaching bit, giving him a guilt trip. It was the kind of talking to that made you wish you were getting the thrashing instead.

The merchants weren't bad people by any means; they just couldn't see that their children were little demons in disguise. They worked hard for what they had, and overall were pretty good people.

Anna McMurray, the mother, was a small woman with mousey-brown hair she kept pulled back so tight that it looked like her eyeballs were going to pop right out of their sockets—kind of scary looking. She actually looked like a Pekinese puppy. She was an average looking woman—except for the popping eyeballs.

Bill McMurray, the father, was also a small-built man, not much bigger than his wife. He had fiery red hair, but no freckles. Since both merchants were slight, everyone secretly wondered why Emilia was so tall.

"Maybe she has a gland problem," the townspeople would whisper to one another.

The eccentric town also boasted a tiny hardware store right beside the mercantile. The hardware store was owned by a young man named John Perkins. He was an outsider to the town and had moved there specifically to open a hardware store. He wasn't very manly at all. He wasn't big or burly or endowed with an impressive presence. Everyone speculated as to why he had come to their small village-like town. The rumors ran from him being a spy for the government to an escaped convict. No matter what John was in his former life outside of Ravenshire, the fact still remained that he was an unremarkable man.

There was another building in the center of the

town, a small grocery store owned by Mary Smith. She and her husband had opened the store many, many years before he died.

As with all others, the speculation about where her husband's money had come from fed the gossip mills. There were rumors that he had been in some kind of shady business, and that he had inherited the money from a rich aunt. The only ones who knew the truth were Samuel Smith and Mary Smith, and Samuel Smith had taken the secret with him to his grave.

As for Mary Smith, she was an accomplished cook. The only reason the good church people would come to the after Sunday service dinners was to have some of whatever she had cooked that day.

Right beside the grocery store was the town pub. It had old wooden, plank floors and the place was decorated in a pirate/sailor type theme, complete with a ship's wheel adorned with wooden spokes. Upstairs above the old pub was where the owner, Sailor Slim Robbins, lived. With Sailor Slim there was little speculation, everyone knew that he had been a sailor before opening the pub. They did, however, question if he had just been a sailor or had Slim been a pirate?

The pub was almost as popular as the church on Sundays. In fact, most of the church members went to the pub to reflect on the busy day over a cool drink. As a show of respect and appreciation, Sailor Slim would attend church on Sunday mornings to give his ten percent tithes and show thanks to God for his good fortune and prosperous business.

Now, you may think that slim was an old man, but he wasn't. He was but a boy when he began his sailing career. Ravenshire was actually his childhood home. You may wonder why a man of such an exciting life would have come back to this tiny town to settle. In order to answer that question, we have to talk about the one-room schoolhouse.

This was one of the few towns that still had a one-room school. It looked kind of like the schoolhouse from *Little House on the Prairie*; only it didn't double as the church. Preacher Norris said that just would not do. He said God's house was God's house only, and he was not going to have mischievous children in there all day disrespecting a place of worship.

The building was small with white-washed siding, two windows on each side, a small wooden door, and a shiny brass bell that hung just outside the door. The bell could be heard twice a day; once in the morning and once right after lunch. There were also a couple of plank swings in a huge maple tree just outside the schoolhouse. Inside, there were ten small school benches, one huge blackboard, a small teacher's desk—piled high with papers and books—and a tiny wood stove.

The town was like a time capsule as the world modernized around them. The only modern influence was the indoor plumbing and the gas-generated electricity. Unfortunately, very few had those luxuries.

The schoolteacher of this traditional one-room schoolhouse, one of the few remaining, was Slim's one true love. They had loved each other as children and it broke the schoolteacher's heart when Slim left as a boy.

The teacher's name was Becky Bingham. She had waited all those years for old Slim to come back and, low and behold, he did. Even though Slim was her beau and he had asked her many times to become Mrs. Sailor Slim Robbins, she had never said yes.

Then there was John "Doc" Dellinger (not to be mistaken with the infamous bank robber), who was the

Ravenshire doctor for more than 50 years.. He was a kind, generous and well respected man. He would often barter and trade for his services. However, he never married and never had children. He always said that he was married to the town and the townspeople were his children.

He had a simple office in a tiny room in the front of his home. There he kept his stethoscope, the light he wore on his head to aid his increasingly aging sight, alcohol, and medicines in blue bottles and brown bottles, all of his tools of the trade. His office was never in disarray. An abundance of sunlight shone in through a large window in the front of his office beside the entrance and an overpowering scent of alcohol filled the room.

There wasn't a day that passed that Doc Dellinger did not receive a patient—even if they were simply bringing him a pie, a dozen eggs, or even a handmade quilt to show thanks for his kindness. He would thank them and simply say, "You are all my children, I must care for you."

Finally, there was the Frye Family who lived in the gleaming glass house on the outskirts of town up on a ridge that overlooked Ravenshire. Their kindness and generosity was extended to everyone in their town. Not only did they lend helping hands in repairing the schoolhouse, but also purchased the brass bell—it was not just any bell, it was the most exquisite bell money could buy.

Even though the kindness and generosity of the Frye family well exceeded any other in Ravenshire, this did not exempt them from the gossiping rumor mill. There was great speculation as to how the Fryes came to own an exuberant amount of land in Ravenshire. The simple fact was that Ernest Frye's family and his wife, Ruby's family had settled Ravenshire after the Ravens did. They had homesteaded the land before a town was even dreamed about.

Preacher Norris and the Church

Preacher Norris not only believed in only having the best for God's house, but also for the parsonage. After all, he was the preacher delivering God's word, so neither the church nor Preacher Norris ever went without the very best.

The good folks of Ravenshire never questioned Preacher Norris or his motives—to his face. Behind his back, however, everyone complained and gossiped. Rumor had it that Preacher Norris had been a pastor at a church in Glenbrook and he was dismissed because he hadn't been honest about how he spent the tithes.

Preacher Norris had first set foot in the simple town of Glenbrook to attend one of their renowned revivals. It was

Ravenshire

a huge revival; there were preachers and musicians from several neighboring towns attending. Preacher Norris had passed himself off as a faith healer. To the amazement of the town, many of the sick people were healed by him. After his wonderful performance, the town decided they needed him to lead their congregation. Without any warning, they sent their preacher packing—the very man who had organized the wonderful revival. To the townspeople's disappointment, Preacher Norris had no further luck at healing the sick after the revival.

In the small town of Glenbrook he only had the best for himself and the church. It didn't take long for the townspeople to see that the only good thing about Preacher Norris was watching him walk away, so they sent him packing as well—called his crime against the church and God a misappropriation of funds.

It was rumored that the church was without a

replacement for almost a year before another preacher accepted the position. That was fine with the town; they made do with what they had—traveling preachers passing through, guest preachers from other churches and sometimes they just had musical services.

It wasn't long after Glenbrook had dismissed him until the good Preacher Norris came upon the sleepy community of Ravenshire. As luck would have it—for the preacher—Ravenshire was in need of a man of the cloth.

The townspeople of Ravenshire were not blinded by the preacher, they just had no other choice. Because Ravenshire was so behind in the times—which was how they preferred it—they couldn't get anyone else to take the position. They listened to him preach, taking the best and leaving the rest from his sermons.

Poor old Preacher Norris thought he had the town hoodwinked. Little did he know that they were keeping a watchful eye on him.

The McMurrays

What more can be said about the McMurrays—quite a bit. In fact, pretty much everyone in the tiny town of Ravenshire had a secret or two and a lot to be said about them. The McMurrays were no exception. That was probably why the town didn't say much to Preacher Norris about his less than honest behavior.

The McMurrays tried to be good people and good parents. There was a reason behind that. Anna was betrothed to another and Bill did a few dishonest things to win her heart and Anna was easily swayed.

Anna was being courted by a man named Bartholomew who owned a very profitable funeral home he had inherited when his father died. He was a handsome young man with dark hair, a strong build, and deep brown eyes. Everyone in town knew they would eventually marry since they had been sweethearts from childhood, but Bill McMurray had other ideas.

Bill was not a bad person, just a bit misguided. He was in love and he was certain that Bartholomew did not love Anna as much as he did. So when his opportunity arose, he jumped on the chance to win his fair Anna.

Bartholomew had been thrown by his horse and was bedridden for about six months. Bill stepped in to help him with his business while Bartholomew was on the mends. Everything seemed fine in the beginning and Bartholomew appreciated Bill's help. He was sure that without Bill's help, his business would have no doubt suffered.

Bill offered to help Anna out around her place too, becoming increasingly friendly with her parents. Soon Bill was the hero in town and Bartholomew was all but forgotten in the town's eyes.

Finally, it occurred to Bill exactly how to complete his plan. He went out of town on a business trip, only this was not your typical business trip. Bill went to see a big shot lawyer in a neighboring town. He was no ordinary lawyer, he was more of a—well, swindler. For a hefty payment he would do pretty much anything asked of him.

Bill asked him to draw up an agreement that would appear to be an ordinary contract with a company for providing caskets. However, there was so much hidden language and mumbo-jumbo that no one but a lawyer would be able to tell it was indeed a contract that gave Bill the funeral home for the work he had done for Bartholomew. The company was created for Bill just for the sole purpose of stealing the funeral home right out from under Bartholomew.

So he headed back to Ravenshire with the contract

in his greedy hand. He went straight to see Bartholomew and showed him the new and wonderful contract that would increase his business. Bartholomew was eager to sign the contract and Bill tucked it away for a future day. It was only another month before Bartholomew was back on his feet and ready to take control of his business once again.

The day he decided he could face work, he went to Bill who was already hard at work at the funeral home.

"Good morning, Bill," Bartholomew said with a huge smile.

"Well, well, well. What have we here? Bartholomew, as I live and breathe, you have decided to finally show up for work. I thought I would surely need to fire you for missing so much work," Bill replied.

Bartholomew laughed. "Oh, Bill, you always were the funny one. Seriously, thank you for handling everything for me but I can take everything over now."

"Well, no you can't," Bill said.

"Okay, enough with the jokes. I'm going to my office if anyone should need me," Bartholomew said, becoming a little perturbed. He ran his fingers through his hair and rubbed the back of his neck as he turned to walk away.

Bill grabbed Bartholomew's arm with one hand and pulled out the contract with the other hand. He shoved it under Bartholomew's nose.

"What's this?" Puzzled, Bartholomew looked at Bill.

"This is the contract you signed giving me the funeral home for all the work I have done here."

"What! I did no such thing! Bill, what are you talking about? Surely you are jesting."

"No, get a lawyer to read it for you. This is the

contract that you signed about a month ago," Bill explained.

"No, the contract I signed was to provide caskets for that company—what was the name?"

"Jonathan Enterprises—William Jonathan McMurray is the owner," Bill stated plainly and proudly as he leaned back and crossed his arms.

"Billy, you would do this to your own brother?" Bartholomew asked with tears in his eyes.

"I'm sorry, Bart, but I am in love with Anna and I knew that I could never compete with your looks and money. But I thought if I could level the playing field I could win her over. You always had everything you wanted. I had nothing. You were the oldest so you got the family business. I was left out in the cold with nothing."

Bartholomew knew his brother was extremely

thorough and smart and he could not fight him in court. He conceded his loss. Bill was right, as soon as Anna discovered that Bill was the new owner of the McMurray Funeral Parlor she dumped poor Bartholomew and set her sights on Bill.

Bartholomew left town and never spoke to his brother or Anna again. Bill wanted to own his own business but not one that Bartholomew had, so he closed the funeral parlor and tore down the building. He rebuilt the mercantile on the land and started his own business. He and Anna eventually married and had children.

Bill and Anna did really love each other and were probably meant to be together, but the way it came about made them both very remorseful. They tried to contact Bartholomew several times to mend their relationships with him, but he never returned their letters.

Their regret made them strive to be better people.

However, in their attempt to be good people they ended up spoiling their children and causing problems for many.

John Perkins

John Perkins, the owner of the hardware store, had moved to Ravenshire from the city. No one in Ravenshire knew why John had decided to make his home there. Many rumors swirled, but no one ever asked him. He was shy and wasn't very well at conversing with others. For this reason, the people of Ravenshire thought him to be rude.

John also had a story to tell, but he chose to keep it to himself. John was born and raised in the city and liked where he lived until the day things went wrong. He had been a bank manager in the city and enjoyed his job more than anything else in his life until that one lazy afternoon when she walked in—Bianca Lupei.

It was love at first sight for John. Bianca was not

blind and could see how much John liked her; she had plans for such a man.

Bianca was beautiful with raven-black hair styled in the fashion of the day—a short bob cut. She had the bluest eyes that anyone had ever seen, wore the most stylish clothes, and to top it off she had a beautiful foreign accent.

John was a small man with mousy brown hair and dark eyes. He was average looking and by no means handsome, but not ugly either. He just did not have much luck with women so when Bianca gave him attention he instantly became a slave to her every whim.

Their relationship blossomed over the months and John was head over heels in love with her. The day finally came that John asked Bianca to marry him. He took her on a wonderful picnic and when they sat down to eat Bianca was presented with the most beautiful diamond engagement ring. It sparkled like stars in the sky on a clear winter night.

"Bianca, will you marry me," John timidly asked, feeling like he might be sick.

Bianca knew it was time to put her plan into action. She was delighted at the proposal.

"Of course, John. I would love to be your wife. But how would we possibly live? You don't make nearly enough money to support us, and I am certain that my father would not give us his blessing without a large dowry. What ever shall we do?" she replied in her accent that made John's knees go weak as she pouted with sultry lips, and batted her eyes at him.

"Well, I'm not sure. I had not considered a dowry; I spent every penny that I had ever saved on the ring." He looked at the ground in disappointment.

Bianca let the tears roll. "Oh, John, I would love to say yes, but I cannot without my father's permission. And should he decide on someone else before you have the dowry, I should be married away right out from under you." Bianca seemed to weep beyond control.

John was so distraught they ended their picnic early. He put the ring back in his pocket and took Bianca home. He returned to his small, modest apartment where he paced the floor all night. Creak after creak of the wooden floorboards under each step he could hear her words echoing in his head—*Dowry, Dowry, Dowry.* What could he possibly do to get a substantial dowry for Bianca's hand in marriage?

John had a small safe in his apartment that he had hidden in the wall behind a picture. He opened the safe as if hoping to find some miracle he had overlooked—maybe he had more stashed away than he had thought, maybe it was hiding in the back of the safe. But no luck. The safe was empty with the exception of his birth certificate.

Sadly, he shut the safe without bothering to hang

the picture back up. John sat down on the scratchy, second-hand couch and just stared at the safe. Then he had an idea. It was not the greatest idea he had ever had; he knew there would be consequences if things did not go as planned. He went to devising his scheme.

The next morning John went to see Bianca.

As soon as she answered the door he said, "Pack your bags. We will be leaving before noon today. Your father will have his dowry and you will be my wife. You will be rich and I will have the money to support us. No questions, just be at the train station by eleven."

"What are you planning, John?" Bianca asked, knowing good and well what he was planning. It was what she had wanted since the day she met him in the bank.

"Let's just say we will be rich, and I will no longer have a job at the bank. Now go and do as I say," John quickly kissed her and headed to the bank.

When he arrived at work, everything was as it was every other day—everything but one. This day John would leave for lunch and never return. He greeted his co-workers like he did every morning, but this time he went in his office and closed the door. He pulled out some large files from his filing cabinet. With files in hand, he opened his office door and headed to the vault.

Susan, a young teller bumped into him. "Mr. Perkins, where are you headed off to?"

"Um—well I have to check on some funds that came in a few days ago." He held the files up and smiled sheepishly at her.

"Okay, do you need help?"

"No! I mean, no, that's alright. I have it under control. You can go on to your station. Thank you anyway," he said.

"Okay," Susan said as she took a deep breath and rolled her eyes at him. "If you change your mind let me know."

"I will, thank you," John said as he proceeded to the safe and Susan returned to her station.

John went into the vault and emptied the files into an empty bag he had hidden beneath his suit jacket, and then hid the bag under a shelf that was stacked with money. He took out stacks of money from a bag in the vault and laid them in the files, closed and arranged it to look like his paperwork. He quickly went back to his office where he put the files into his empty briefcase. There must have been three million dollars in it. He put his briefcase under his desk and did his work as usual, helping the tellers, helping customers, and even issuing a loan.

Ten Forty-Five rolled around and he told everyone that he was having an early lunch with Bianca and had to leave. He stopped at his apartment, put half of the money is his suitcase for him and Bianca to start a new life with, and left the rest in his briefcase to give to her father. John went to the train station where he found his lovely Bianca awaiting.

"Hello, Love," John said as he approached Bianca.

He was so excited to be embarking on his new life with Bianca and frightened they would be found out before escaping. He palms were sweating and his heart pounded as he scanned the station for authorities. He did not want to spend the rest of his life wearing black and white stripes working on the chain gang.

"Jonathan, what is going on?"

"We are going to leave this place and be married. I have the dowry; it's here in my briefcase. Do you think one and a half million is enough?"

Bianca could barely contain her excitement. "Well, yes. I believe it is."

"Okay, so where does your father live? We need to buy tickets and leave on the next train out."

"He lives in New Brook. You buy the tickets; I need to use the washroom. Would you like for me to take the briefcase—just in case there is suspicion?"

"Well, yes that would be fine. I will buy the tickets and you meet me on the platform."

Bianca leaned over and gave Jonathan a kiss on the cheek. "I will," she said.

She turned and walked to the washroom. However, when Jonathan turned to purchase the tickets, she quickly made her way across the room to the platform where she got on the eleven-fifteen to Green Haven, which was in the opposite direction of New Brook. She had anticipated

Jonathan robbing his own bank and him trusting her with the money.

She had purchased her ticket as soon as she had arrived. She found her seat in the cabin with her real fiancé and partner in crime. They quietly awaited departure, hidden so that Jonathan could not find her.

Jonathan searched the train station until his train was ready to depart. Realizing that he had been taken, sadly he boarded his train to New Brook. He knew he had to disappear for good unless he wanted to spend the rest of his life in jail. As luck would have it, he heard a man talking about a small town called Ravenshire. Jonathan was intrigued and thought this would be the perfect place to disappear. When he reached New Brook, he purchased a ticket to the closest town to Ravenshire that had a train station. From there he took a coach to his new home.

Since he still had the surprise money for Bianca—

the money they were to live on—he bought a piece of land and opened the hardware store. He was saddened that Bianca had betrayed and used him.

Mary Smith

Everyone in Ravenshire thought that Mary Smith's husband, Samuel, had either come into his money in some shady manner or he had inherited the money from a dead relative. This was not the case. You see, Samuel was not the one who had acquired their fortune; it was Mary. There was a reason everyone in town loved Mary's cooking. From the time Mary was a little girl, she loved to help her mother in the kitchen, baking pies, breads, and cakes. As a child, Mary's house always smelled of fresh-baked food. When she was finished with her schooling she went off to culinary school in the city.

Mary became a chef and worked in several restaurants—a better restaurant each time, before finally meeting Chef Pierre. He was a famous chef from France.

He had come into the restaurant where Mary was working and ordered a meal; it was second only to his own culinary skills. He had to meet the chef and before long, he and Mary became close friends.

After many months, Chef Pierre decided to open a restaurant in the city. He asked Mary if she would be his partner and she eagerly agreed. They moved to the city; Pierre handled the money and Mary handled the kitchen. It was a wonderful partnership. The restaurant became world-renowned. People would come from everywhere to eat at The Bistro. It was an amazing success catering to the wealthiest and most affluent people.

However, one sunny afternoon a beautiful woman with long golden hair, sea-green eyes, placid skin, and rosy cheeks came into The Bistro and Chef Pierre's world changed forever. This was no ordinary woman; she was a princess. She had come from a far away land just to taste the famous gourmet food from The Bistro.

This beautiful woman walked up to Chef Pierre and introduced herself. "Hello, my name is Princess Alana. I have traveled many days to come here. I would like to meet the famous Chef Pierre."

Chef Pierre held out his hand. "What a pleasure. I am Chef Pierre. Please, come sit."

Chef Pierre pulled out a chair for Princess Alana. "I will fetch you a menu."

"Oh, there's no need for that. You just bring me your best dish," the Princess requested.

Chef Pierre did as Princess Alana asked. She ate her meal while getting to know Chef Pierre. She stayed in town for a few weeks and the two had a whirlwind romance. After only twelve days, Chef Pierre proposed to the princess. They soon married and Chef Pierre was elated.

However, Princess Alana was unhappy sharing Chef Pierre with the world and with Mary. She begged him to sell The Bistro and move to her land and into her palace. Chef Pierre loved his princess so much that he decided he must sell the wonderful restaurant and part ways with both cooking and Mary.

Mary was saddened, but that all changed when The Bistro was sold and she received a small fortune. She then invested her money in other things, such as the railroad and a coal company. It seemed that everything Mary invested in turned to gold. Mary had the King Midas touch. She would never have to worry about finances ever again.

Mary was no longer a chef and had time to venture out, travel to new and exciting places and meet people. One day she decided to take a trip to check on one of her investments, so she traveled to one of her diamond mines; there she met Samuel, a miner. The minute their eyes, met they fell head over heals in love. They, too, had a whirlwind romance and marriage, though not as quick as Chef Pierre and Princess Alana's. They were married in less than a year of meeting.

Just as Princess Alana had requested of Chef Pierre, Samuel begged Mary to leave her hectic life to be only with him. Mary loved Samuel enough to do so, however, she did not sell her shares in her investments. She simply hired someone to conduct her affairs in her place.

Mary and Samuel then decided to move to Ravenshire because it was quaint and quiet and no one knew Mary was rich. There they could live a quiet, peaceful life and Mary could do what she loved: cook.

So now, that is why Mary is such a good cook and that is where Samuel and Mary's fortune came from.

Sailor Slim Robins

Now since everyone knew that Sailor Slim Robins had previously been a sailor, the only speculation was had he been merely a sailor or had he been a pirate. Well the truth of the matter was, Slim had indeed been a pirate.

Slim did not want the town to know about his piracy days. He was bound and determined to marry Becky Bingham and he thought if she knew about his sordid past she would never marry him.

Slim had taken off as a boy to begin his career as a sailor. He had participated in some unscrupulous ventures in order to make enough money to go back to Ravenshire, open a business, and finally marry Becky.

Slim had been all over the world exploring. He had

encountered all kinds of rare sea creatures and had bartered and sold them—even though he made money in piracy, he made most of his money by selling those beautiful creatures. He was so in love with Becky that all he could think about was the quickest way to make money and get back to her.

While sailing on his pirate ship, he came across the rarest of sea creatures—a mermaid. Now had he been a smart man he would have left it be. But his love for Becky blinded him and corrupted his morals. He captured this beautiful mermaid in his fishnet.

He and his men pulled her aboard with ease. They knew little about mermaids and though this mermaid was a beautiful and enchanting creature, she was exceptionally dangerous. She sang her beautiful song and entranced the men on the ship.

When they were least expecting it, her long, sharp

claws protruded from her fingertips and razor sharp teeth replaced her beautiful, pearly whites.

Only one man on the ship was left alive, Slim Robins. Only Slim Robins was in love. His love for Becky caused him to be immune from her song and saved him from the creature. After killing his entire crew, the mermaid once again looked as beautiful and enchanting as before standing amongst the bloody remains of the crew.

She spoke softly to Slim. "You need to give up this terrible thing that you do and go home to your love. Never again take another creature from the sea and their families. You humans think that we don't have feelings or you just don't care. You go back and tell what you have witnessed, never setting sail on my enchanted waters again."

The mermaid turned and flipped off the side of the ship and back into the water. She looked over her shoulder at Slim briefly and then swam away. Slim was terrified. It would take him days to make it back to shore and he had no crew to help him man the ship.

He put the bodies of his crew to rest in the ocean. Saddened, he eventually reached shore. He did as the mermaid had instructed but no one believed his wild story. He didn't care. He also headed back to Becky as the mermaid had instructed. He never again thought about returning to the ocean. He didn't even have a desire to get on a fishing boat or a canoe. Slim had never been a land lover, but he quickly became one on his last voyage.

Becky Bingham

Becky Bingham's story wasn't nearly as exciting as Slim Robins'. Becky and Slim were childhood sweethearts. However, Slim left thinking that he had to make a fortune before Becky would marry him. But when he left, it broke Becky's heart.

Becky had always wanted to be a schoolteacher and after Slim left that's what she did. She was just a girl when Slim set off to seek his fortune. Becky feared that he would never return. Her broken heart turned hard toward true love as she cried in despair every day for an entire year.

When she wiped away that last tear, Becky decided to follow her dream of teaching. This required her to go to a neighboring town to be educated for the simple fact that

Ravenshire hadn't had a teacher in a few years. While Becky was away she met another, Michael Matthews. She was surprised when this young man won over her heart.

In the bright, sunny afternoons of spring he would take Becky on long walks in the town and by the river. One warm summer evening while strolling around town with her white lace parasol shading her beautiful blonde locks, she saw Michael with another young lady. She was devastated when she saw him kiss this woman.

Becky never spoke to Michael again, and she never told anyone back home about Michael. She finished her schooling and swore to herself never to let another man into her heart. At summer's end Becky returned to Ravenshire.

The town spent several weeks before Becky's return repairing the old school in preparation for the new schoolteacher. They patched the roof, tacked back the loose siding, replaced the slate chalkboard, repaired the seats, washed the windows and floors, dusted everywhere, and white-washed the outside. The very last thing they did was to take down the old school bell that had been struck by lightening years before, and replace it with a shiny new one.

A few years earlier, lightning struck the schoolhouse bell during a huge storm and ran onto the front porch of the school, burning it right up. Luckily, it was raining so hard that the rain put the fire out before it burnt the whole schoolhouse down. The first citizens of Ravenshire that were at the schoolhouse the very next morning ready to help was the Frye family. The porch was repaired, but the bell was not replaced.

On the day that Becky returned as the Ravenshire teacher the entire town seemed deserted. The stagecoach stopped in front of the mercantile and Becky stepped down before the coachman handed off her luggage. She was surprised to see that the mercantile was closed. As she looked around, everything was closed and she could spot no one.

Becky was totally stumped. She shrugged her shoulders, picked up her bags, and walked toward the schoolhouse. She was tired of lugging around those school books. Becky thought she would leave them at the schoolhouse and go back the next day to clean and prepare for the students of Ravenshire.

She slowly walked to the door of the schoolhouse feeling lonely and discouraged while kicking at a loose stone. However, she did notice that the school had been freshly whitewashed and the bell looked new. She squinted her eyes as she thought, but couldn't image why this had been done and why no one was around.

Becky shrugged, sat her bags down, and grasped the doorknob. She slowly turned the doorknob and began to push the door open when she was startled by a myriad of familiar voices.

"Surprise!"

With a start, Becky jumped. Even though she felt she had lost her love, Slim, and had been scorned by Michael, she felt as though this school, the children, and the love of the townspeople could help fill the void. She could live as a spinster. Becky smiled and her eyes filled with tears of joy as she looked around at all of the hard work everyone must have put into getting the school ready for her return.

"Oh, my! Everything looks lovely. Thank you all for everything you have done."

The townspeople ushered Becky in and proudly showed her everything they had accomplished. Becky was ready to begin her life—a life that did not include a man. The very next week, Becky opened the doors of the school and all of the children of Ravenshire anxiously attended.

Doc Dellinger

Doc Dellinger was a man of simple means. He was there for everyone and anyone in Ravenshire that needed him or his services.

Doc Dellinger wasn't your typical doctor; he would barter his services if someone was sick and needed to be treated but couldn't pay. They could trade him a few dozen fresh brown chicken eggs, a side of beef, or even baked goods or hand-made quilts.

Everyone in the town revered and respected Doc Dellinger. However, he too had his secrets. When he was a young man, he and his best friend had their eyes set on the same young woman. They decided that a friendly competition would be the way to decide who would get the girl.

They both did their best to woo her. They showered her with gifts, affection, and attention. This young lady, Mary Martin, had no idea at first that they had entered into this competition. However, one day she overheard a conversation between the two young men regarding their friendly competition.

Mary was outraged and sent them both packing. John went to Mary's home and knocked on her door. Her mother answered.

"May I speak to Mary? I need to explain something to her," John begged as he fidgeted with his hat.

Mary's mother called up the stairs to Mary, "Mary, John is here to see you."

Mary did not respond, she simply came down the stairs. John could see that her hands were filled with everything that he had given her: flowers, a necklace, a pink scarf, and a tiny glass figurine of a doll. She walked up to him with pain in her eyes and an angry look upon her face.

"John take these things and leave my sight. I wish to never see nor her from you again. Do not say a word. Just leave."

Mary shoved the items in his hands and slammed the door in his face.

John did as she asked. With tears in his eyes he turned and left, never to bother her again. He took these precious items and placed them in a small wooden box with lilies carved in the top. He kept this box hidden away in a dresser drawer. John would take this box out on occasion and examine its contents, but not often because it always made him melancholy.

Little did Mary know that John Dellinger really

loved her and would have walked the ends of the earth to please her. He loved her so much that the guilt he had for deceiving her was more than he could bear. He wanted to make up for this terrible thing that he had done, so he decided to become a doctor so he could help others. John went to medical school and drowned his sorrows in his studies.

When he became a doctor, he did not return to his hometown but went somewhere where no one knew of him or how his actions had hurt the only woman he would ever love. So he moved to a little town that was in dire need of a doctor, Ravenshire. He did so much good for the people of Ravenshire that he more than made up for the pain he had caused Mary.

Mary had really loved John and was so hurt by him that she was unable to trust another man. Poor Mary never married. She had many suitors, but her response never wavered as she sternly told them that she was not interested.

The Frye Family

The Frye family was a bit different than the others in Ravenshire. There were five children whom the townspeople called the Glass House children because their house had so many windows held together with gleaming copper it appeared to be made of glass. These children were blessed to have both parents and their grandmother to raise them.

This family lived as one with nature and gave back what they took. They also had special gifts. Some members of the Frye family could see fairies, sprites, nymphs, hearth brownies, etc. All members of the Frye family had some special gift or talent and they owned much of the land in Ravenshire, which gave way to much gossiping in the town.

The Glass House children loved venturing out and were never at a loss for some type of adventure. The children came by this adventurous spirit naturally. Both their mother and father had been that way as children. An adventure they had taken as youngsters is how they came to know about the population of ravens in Ravenshire.

Ma Frye, Ruby, and Pa Frye, Ernest decided they were going to venture out and find where the ravens nested. They had been playing on a rope swing in Ernest's yard when they noticed the ravens flying up above them. They began speculating about the ravens.

Ernest asked Ruby, "Do you know where the ravens live?"

Ruby responded, "No. Do you? Why do you ask?"

"I don't know either. I want to find them. I want to see just how many there are. I bet there are so many that we won't be able to count them all."

"How will we find them?" Ruby asked.

"We will just follow those two who keep circling above. I think they want us to follow them. They have been doing this every day for a week."

"You know, you may be right. I have noticed them a lot this week. Okay, let's follow them," Ruby said, ready for an adventure as she stood and dusted her dress.

Ernest smiled and stood up. He whistled loudly and yelled at the birds. "Hey, we are ready to follow you. So show us where to go."

To their amazement the ravens swooped down, almost touching the children. They laughed as they blinked their eyes and dodged the birds. The ravens then flew low to the ground and slowly so the children could easily follow.

Ernest and Ruby followed the ravens through beautiful plush green meadows, across a dusty and brown rocky mountain cliff, and through clear, cool streams until they eventually found themselves in the midst of thousands of ravens deep within a forest. The ravens were all squawking as though they were all jabbering to one another at the same time.

When the raven colony noticed the children they all gathered around them and continued their jabbering, only this time it appeared that they were squawking at the children. Ruby and Ernest were very surprised at how friendly the ravens seemed to be.

After a few minutes, the squawking of the ravens began to sound like words. Then there were no longer bird noises, only words—a myriad of words. The children could not understand what the ravens were saying because they were all speaking at once.

Out of the blue a massive white raven came from deep within the forest and landed at the children's feet.

"Quiet!" he yelled out to the other ravens.

The others immediately quieted in a show of respect.

"Well, it's about time. I thought I would surely die from old age before you two finally made your way here. What took you so long?"

Ernest and Ruby looked at one another in astonishment. Finally Ernest spoke, "We didn't know you wanted to see us. We just saw the ravens this morning and decide to try to find where you all lived."

Ruby asked, "What do you need from us?"

The white raven responded, "I need you to know why we are here so that you can help us. We have been brought here by the Nature Goddess to protect the fairy folk. It has been shown to me in a dream that you will one day be married and your lands will be joined. The fairy folk are hidden on these lands and you will be responsible for making sure that no one disturbs them."

Ernest responded, "I don't know about us getting married, but I can promise that I will make sure they are safe on the Frye land."

Ruby agreed, "I will also make sure that they are protected on the Thompson land."

"Very well. Now I believe that my children have many questions for you. Will you stay and speak with them?"

The children were thrilled at the old raven's request. "Of course will we," Ruby answered.

So Ruby and Ernest spent the entire evening with the ravens. They went back often, even as adults. They kept a close friendship with the ravens their entire life, and kept their promise to the Ravens by protecting the lands and the fairy folk.

The townspeople of Ravenshire never understood why there were so many ravens in the town, but the Frye family did. This was their secret.